JAN 1 3 2011

W9-BQV-464

Crayon
marks noted
← CS 12/15/11

The Lunchbox

A humorous
rhyming story

This edition first published in 2010 by
Sea-to-Sea Publications
Distributed by Black Rabbit Books
P.O. Box 3263, Mankato, Minnesota 56002

Text and illustration © Jane Cope 2006, 2010

Printed in USA

Library of Congress Cataloging-in-Publication Data

Cope, Jane.
  The lunchbox / written and illustrated by Jane Cope.
      p. cm. -- (Reading corner)
  Summary: Tired of his mother's homemade lunches but wary of buying school
dinners, George is thrilled to have his aunt fill his new lunchbox with treats for a
week, but on Friday he learns that what tastes good sometimes leads to trouble.
  ISBN 978-1-59771-250-7 (hardcover)
  [1. Stories in rhyme. 2. Luncheons--Fiction. 3. Food--Fiction.] I. Title.
  PZ8.3.C798Lun 2010
  [E]--dc22
                            2008051355

9 8 7 6 5 4 3 2

Published by arrangement with the Watts Publishing Group Ltd., London

Series Editor: Jackie Hamley
Series Advisors: Dr. Linda Gambrell, Dr. Barrie Wade, Dr. Hilary Minns
Series Designer: Peter Scoulding

For Tom and Ian—J.C.

The
Lunchbox

Written and illustrated by
Jane Cope

SEA-TO-SEA
Mankato Collingwood London

Jane Cope

"My son, Tom, was the inspiration for this story— I made an awful lot of packed lunches for him that never got eaten! I often illustrate other people's stories, but it was great fun to do all the words and pictures myself. I really loved drawing Aunt Peg because she's so big and colorful."

Monday morning was always a rush.

"Yuck!" shouted Mom

as she washed out the mush

from last Friday's lunchbox.

"Now listen, George, please.

What's it to be, tuna salad or cheese?"

"Neither," said George.

"That cheese makes me sick.

And you always make sandwiches

so horribly thick!

"I'm tired of taking that lunchbox
to school!
Why can't you buy me
a new one that's cool?"

7

"Well, I'm tired of making your
lunches!" said Mom.

"School cafeteria's the answer!"

George looked very glum.

"Now you know until Friday
I'm going away.
So Aunt Peg will be making
your lunch every day.

"Is that all right?" Mom asked,

shutting the door.

"Great!" replied George,

"I like her food more!"

On Tuesday at eight,
Mom let Aunt Peg in.
"George!" cried Aunt Peg,
"you're looking so thin!

I've bought you a lunchbox,
isn't it cool?"
"Fantastic!" said George.
"I'll take it to school!"

13

Into the lunchbox
went chips...

a sweet pastry...

and three cans of soda.
It was all very tasty!

"I'll soon fatten you up!"
said the smiling Aunt Peg,
as she picked off a cherry
that stuck to her leg.

On Wednesday Peg made
a huge sandwich pile:
peanut butter with chocolate—
it took quite a while!

"You see, Georgie,

food is one of the arts!"

And in case he got hungry,

she popped in six tarts.

On Thursday the lunchbox was
bursting with pies.
"I made some with molasses,
as a special surprise.

"And tomorrow," said Peg,

"will be our last lunch.

So I'll make sure you have

something yummy to munch!"

On Friday at lunch,

George's friends kept on gazing.

The colorful mix was just

so amazing...

Shocking shrimp twirls and
marshmallow whoppers,
blue fizzy drinks and
crackly corn poppers.

21

George munched,
he crunched...

he crammed,
and he slurped.

He nibbled and stuffed...

he gulped...

and he
burped.

CLANG! went the bell.

Children jumped to their feet.

And slowly George eased himself

out of his seat.

He felt hot...

he felt cold...

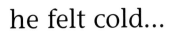

he felt rather weird.
He turned a bit green,
then just as he feared...

WHOOSH! Up it all came,

the whole sugary bunch.

A great rainbow fountain—

he threw up his whole lunch!

There were squeals and shrieks
and quite a to-do.
"Ugh! Yuck! Look, teacher,
it's all over my shoe!"

Mom picked George up early
and gave him a hug.
She wondered what caused him
to have such a bug.

"It's not fair," George thought,
"life just isn't easy
when good things are bad
and make you feel queasy."

And later on,
snuggled up cozy in bed,
George said that he might
like Mom's lunches instead.

Notes for parents and teachers

READING CORNER has been structured to provide maximum support for new readers. The stories may be used by adults for sharing with young children. Primarily, however, the stories are designed for newly independent readers, whether they are reading these books in bed at night, or in the reading corner at school or in the library.

Starting to read alone can be a daunting prospect. READING CORNER helps by providing visual support and repeating words and phrases, while making reading enjoyable. These books will develop confidence in the new reader, and encourage a love of reading that will last a lifetime.

If you are reading this book with a child, here are a few tips:

1. Make reading fun. Choose a time to read when you and the child are relaxed and have time to share the story.

2. Encourage children to reread the story, and to retell the story in their own words, using the illustrations to remind them what has happened.

3. Give praise. Remember that small mistakes need not always be corrected.

READING CORNER covers three grades of early reading ability, with three levels at each grade. Each level has a certain number of words per story, indicated by the number of bars on the spine of the book, to allow you to choose the right book for a young reader:

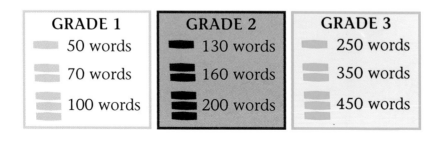

GRADE 1	GRADE 2	GRADE 3
50 words	130 words	250 words
70 words	160 words	350 words
100 words	200 words	450 words